LEAP

WRITTEN BY **CAMPBELL MANNING**

ILLUSTRATED BY **NADIA RONQUILLO**

Designed by Flowerpot Press
in Franklin, TN.
www.FlowerpotPress.com
Designer: Stephanie Meyers
Editor: Katrine Crow
DJS-0912-0157
ISBN: 978-1-4867-0948-9
Made in China/Fabriqué en Chine

Maybe not now,
but pretty soon,
I'm going to LEAP
off of the moon!

I thought I'd jump
off of a star.
For my first time,
that seemed too far.

My friends all laugh.
    They call me nuts.
They say that I
    don't have the guts.

Nobody thinks
my plan will work.
They think my brain
has gone BERSERK!

But I'll show them.
I know I can!
Soon they'll all see
that I'M THE MAN!

And I'm not scared,
no, not one bit.
I'll prove it soon
—I'm doin' it!

A normal plane
    can't make the trip.
I'll have to build
    a rocket ship!

Not any ship
    will do the trick.
It must be big
    and really quick.

I'll need to get
    outer space stuff.
I hope that I
    can find enough.

I hear it's cold, but here's the thing,
    I have long underwear to bring.

And I will need a warm coat, too.
    My furry, fluffy one might do.

And so that I can breathe up there,
I'll bring a zillion cans of air.

I'll bring some spaceman snacks as well.
I will get hungry. I can tell.

Now I'm all set.
    My ship's all packed.
The tank is full.
    Supplies are stacked.

And I'm not one
   to brag or gloat,
but when I reach
   the moon, I'll float!

I'll see the Earth from way up high
and satellites as they pass by.

Stars shining brighter than before,
up where the universe can roar!

These memories
are mine to keep.
I'll lock them in
and then I'll

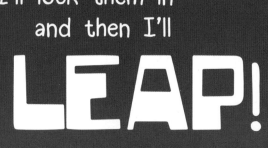

Then falling down
through outer space,
I'll have a grin
upon my face.

And when I reach
the atmosphere,
I'll know the time
is almost here.

Sailing swiftly,
    through sun and clouds,
I will AMAZE
    the giant crowds!

And after I
    have flown and soared,
I'll just lie back
    and PULL THE CORD!

The crowd won't make
    a single sound
as I float down
    and touch the ground.

And then they'll cheer
and scream and cry,
"Did you just see
that HERO FLY?!?"

OH!

Just one last thing:
I have a hunch
Mom makes me wait
'til after lunch.